P9-BYT-119

LOUTTIT LIBRARY
274 Victory Highway
West Greenwich, RI 02817

DISCARDED
by
Louttit Library

The Berenstain Bears

AND THE BIG

SPELLING BEE

LOUTTIT LIBRARY
274 Victory Highway
West Greenwich, RI 02817

When it's Spelling Bee time
at Bear Country School,
the pressure builds up
and it's hard to keep cool!

The Berenstain Bears

AND THE BIG SPELLING BEE

Stan and Jan Berenstain
with Mike Berenstain

HarperFestival®
A Division of HarperCollinsPublishers

The Berenstain Bears and the Big Spelling Bee
Copyright © 2007 by Berenstain Bears, Inc.
HarperCollins®, ▰®, and HarperFestival® are trademarks of
HarperCollins Publishers. All rights reserved. Manufactured in China.
No part of this book may be used or reproduced in any manner
whatsoever without written permission except in the case of brief quotations
embodied in critical articles and reviews. For information address
HarperCollins Children's Books, a division of HarperCollins Publishers,
1350 Avenue of the Americas, New York, NY 10019.
Library of Congress catalog card number: 2006929492
ISBN-10: 0-06-057386-4 (pbk.)—ISBN-13: 978-0-06-057386-7 (pbk.)
ISBN-10: 0-06-057402-X (trade bdg.)—ISBN-13: 978-0-06-057402-4 (trade bdg.)
www.harpercollinschildrens.com
❖
First Edition

Brother and Sister Bear were pretty good students. Like most cubs, they had their strengths and weaknesses. Brother was good at math and science, but sometimes he had trouble with language arts. Sister, on the other hand, had trouble with math and science, but got straight As in language arts.

Sister also read a lot and liked to write stories.

Once, there were three chipmunks.
Their names were Acorn, Peanut, and...

She also happened to be a very good speller.

There are two ways to become a good speller.

One is to study lists of words and memorize the way they are spelled.

The other is to be a good reader and just let the words seep into your brain.

Gwen, a classmate of Sister's, won the big school spelling bee last year. She was expected to win again.

But something surprising happened.

First, there were class spelling bees, which led to the big school spelling bee.

"Now everybody stand at your seats," said Teacher Jane. "I'll give out the words and you'll try to spell them. If you get a word right, you remain standing and wait for your next turn. If you spell it wrong, you sit down."

The words were pretty hard, and soon everyone in the class except Gwen and Sister was sitting down. Sister couldn't believe she was now tied with Gwen, the best speller in the class.

"Treachery," said Teacher Jane. "An act of betrayal."

"Treachery," said Gwen. "T-R-E-C-H-E-R-Y. Treachery."

"That is incorrect," said Teacher Jane. "Please sit down."

Teacher Jane turned to Sister. She was the last one standing.
"Treachery," said Teacher Jane. "An act of betrayal."
"Treachery," said Sister. "T-R-E-A-C-H-E-R-Y. Treachery."
"That is correct," said Teacher Jane. "You have won the warm-up round of the annual Bear County School Spelling Bee."

Sister found herself being congratulated from all sides.

"I didn't know you were such a good speller," said Teacher Jane.

"Neither did I," said Sister.

"You know what this means," said Teacher Jane. "It means you will represent our class in the school spelling bee next Tuesday in the auditorium, and after that . . . "

"Next Tuesday?" said Sister. "But I have an important soccer practice next Tuesday. I'm just junior varsity, but we have to get the varsity ready for a big game."

Teacher Jane just smiled.

"I wouldn't worry about that," she said. "There will be a lot more soccer practices, but there's just one school spelling bee."

It's fun to win, thought Sister. *But I sure hate missing that practice.*

Sister was heading for the playground. She had a date to jump rope with Lizzy and Jill. They met at the playground gate.

"Congratulations!" said Lizzy.

"For what?" asked Sister.

"For winning your class spelling bee, of course."

"How did you hear about it so soon?" asked Sister.

"Good news travels fast," said Lizzy.

"I'm not so sure it's good news," said Sister.

"The school spelling bee is on Tuesday, so I'm going to miss an important soccer practice."

"There'll be a lot more soccer practices," said Jill. "But there's only one—"

"I know," said Sister. "There's only one school spelling bee."

By the time Sister got home, the whole family knew she had won the spelling bee. Papa was especially excited about it.

"Congratulations, Sister!" said Papa. "Way to go! It takes me back to when I was the best speller in the school! I used to knock over those spelling bees like tenpins! I guess you realize that if you win the spelling bee, you'll go to the big All-Schools Spelling Bee in Big Bear City!"

But Sister hadn't realized it.

"Now here's what we're going to do," said Papa.

Mama sidled over to Papa and, in a low voice, said, "Dear, could I speak to you for a moment?" She took him by the arm and led him into the dining room. "Now, Papa," said Mama. "I know you're proud of Sister—I am, too—but you mustn't get carried away and put too much pressure on her."

"Me? Carried away? Ridiculous!" protested Papa. "Besides, Sister can handle pressure! She's tough as a nut. She takes after me!" Then Papa went back into the living room.

"Oh, dear!" said Mama.

"Now, Sister," said Papa. "Here's what we're going to do. First I'm going up to the attic and get my old vocabulary lists from school. Then we're gonna drill, drill, drill until you're letter perfect in every word."

Papa headed up to the attic. The lists took some finding, but Papa found them.

Meanwhile, downstairs, there was a knock on the door. Sister answered it. It was Lizzy and Jill.

"Can you come over and play after supper?"

"I'm afraid not, girls," said Papa, who had come down from the attic with his vocabulary lists. "Sister and I are going to be busy preparing for the school spelling bee. The way I see it, we've got a good chance of going to the All-Schools Spelling Bee in Big Bear City."

Papa was as good as his word. Every evening after school Papa drilled Sister on vocabulary words.

"Destitute," said Papa. "Without money or property."
"Destitute," said Sister. "D-E-S-T-I-T-U-T-E."

"Paramount," said Papa. "The uppermost or highest."
"Paramount," said Sister. "P-A-R-A-M-O-U-N-T."

"Prehistoric," said Papa. "Of that period before recorded history."
"Prehistoric," said Sister. "P-R-E-H-I-S-T-O-R-I-C."

It was Tuesday and the spelling bee was under way. The contestants were up on the stage. There were seven of them. The auditorium was filled with cubs and parents. Papa was there, of course. He was rooting for Sister like crazy.

Mr. Honeycomb, the school principal, was giving out the words. The words were like rockets going off and exploding into bad spelling that knocked out the contestants one by one.

It was down to two cubs: Sister and a fifth-grader.

"Vicarious," said Mr. Honeycomb. "Taking undue pleasure from the achievements of others."

"Vicarious," said the fifth grader. "V-I-C-C-A-R-I-E-S-S, vicarious."

"That is incorrect!" said Mr. Honeycomb. He turned to Sister, who was the last cub standing.

Vicarious, thought Papa out in the audience, *taking undue pleasure from the achievements of others. Good grief! That's exactly what I am doing!*

"Vicarious," said Mr. Honeycomb. "Taking undue pleasure from the achievements of others."

"Vicarious," said Sister. "V-I-C-A-R-I-O-U-S. Vicarious."

"Correct!" cried Mr. Honeycomb, "which means that Sister Bear will be going to the All-Schools Spelling Bee in Big Bear City!"

Sister got a standing ovation, except for Papa, who remained seated.

"How about a little victory snack at the Burger Bear?" said Mama as they left the school.

"Fine," said Papa.

"Sure thing," said Brother.

Sister didn't say anything. She was lost in thought.

"Er, Papa," she said, "I don't know how to say this, and I don't want to disappoint you, but I don't want to go to the All-Schools Spelling Bee in Big Bear City. I just want to go to school, play soccer, and do things with my friends."

"Disappoint me?" said Papa. "You could never disappoint me. In fact, I'm very proud of you for having the courage to stand up for yourself. Tell you what: Why don't you just take off and play with your friends?"

"Oh, may I? I love you, Papa!" And she was gone.

"How about me?" asked Brother. "Cousin
Fred's got a game going over at the ball field."
"Take off," said Papa.

Papa turned to Mama, "Do you
still want to go for a snack?" he asked.
"I don't think so," said Mama. "Let's
just go home and have a cup of tea."

And that's what they did.

10/07

LOUTTIT LIBRARY W. GREENWICH, RI

3 6002 00032 5161

DISCARDED
by
Louttit Library

DATE DUE

NO 06 '07	FEB 04 2015	
NO 24 '07		
NO 30 '07	MAR 03 2015	
MR 27		
MY 06		
DE 16		
FE 27		
APR 02 2009		
JY 07		
AUG 04		
FEB 26		
JUN 0 4 2011		
AUG 01		
AUG 25		
APR 23		
JUL 31		
AUG 01 2014		
GAYLORD		PRINTED IN U.S.A.